P9-DGR-307

CHADRON (NE) STATE COLLEGE
3 5086 00389893 7

NED FELDMAN, SPACE PIRATE

NED FELDMAN, SPACE PIRATE

written and illustrated by

DANIEL PINKWATER

Macmillan Publishing Company New York
Maxwell Macmillan Canada Toronto
Maxwell Macmillan International New York Oxford Singapore Sydney

To JILL

 Macmillan Publishing Company is part of the Maxwell Communication Group of Companies. Macmillan Publishing Company, 866 Third Avenue, New York, NY 10022. Maxwell Macmillan Canada, Inc., 1200 Eglinton Avenue East, Suite 200, Don Mills, Ontario M3C 3N1. First edition. Printed in the United States of America. The text of this book is set in 12 point Aster. The illustrations are rendered in pen and ink with colored markers. 10 9 8 7 6 5 4 3 2 1

Library of Congress Cataloging-in-Publication Data
Pinkwater, Daniel Manus, date. Ned Feldman, space pirate / written and illustrated by Daniel Pinkwater. — 1st ed. p. cm. Summary: One day when Ned's parents are out, he meets Captain Lumpy Lugo, a space pirate who comes from the galaxy Foon-ping-baba, and they spend the afternoon traveling through outer space. ISBN 0-02-774633-X
[1. Extraterrestrial beings—Fiction. 2. Science fiction. 3. Humorous stories.] I. Title.
PZ7.P6335Ne 1994 [E]—dc20 93-40893

CONTENTS

Trees are our friends
They grow in the earth
Some trees have fruit,
others have nuts They
provide homes for many
creatures

Max

1.
Something's Under the Sink

I am Ned Feldman. I am a good student, although I do not always get the best grades. This is because I sometimes hand in homework late. Also, I like to draw pictures of space battles on the margins of my papers. And—my handwriting is horrible. My teacher, Mr. Molloy, gives lower marks for horrible handwriting and pictures of space battles. Mr. Molloy believes in neatness.

I remind Mr. Molloy that my spelling is excellent, and I make great sentences.

He says, "How can I tell? I can hardly read this stuff with the awful writing and the spaceships all over!"

I refuse to let Mr. Molloy discourage me. If I were a teacher, I would be glad to get some papers with nice drawings of space battles. I admit he is right about turning in homework late, and the horrible handwriting. I have promised to work on that. But the space battles stay.

My parents agree with Mr. Molloy, of course. They believe in neatness, too. They talk to me a lot about my room. I am supposed to keep my room neat. This subject comes up almost every day.

Since I became nine years old, my parents have left me home alone now and then. They say I am old enough to be alone in the apartment for an hour or two—and I am. I can handle it. It's no big deal. I like being home alone. If there is a phone call, I write down a message. I am in charge. My parents always tell me where they can be reached if I need them—or I can call my grandma. As I said, it's no big deal.

This particular time, I was alone in the apartment. I was reading a book of amazing stories about space exploration. After a while, I got thirsty and went to the kitchen to get a glass of water.

I like water with ice cubes in it. I had put the ice cubes in the glass and was just about to fill it when I heard a noise.

The noise came from the cabinet under the kitchen sink. Right away, I knew that something alive had made the noise. It was the sound of something moving.

"Wow!" I thought. "There's something alive under the kitchen sink!"

Right away, I thought about what it could be. It sounded too big for a mouse. "Maybe a rat!" I thought. "Maybe a kitten is under there, or a cute baby raccoon, or a big snake—a rattlesnake, ready to strike!"

But I had not heard a rattle. The sound hadn't been a squeak like a mouse's, or a meow. It was just a sound. I couldn't tell what it was.

Then I heard another sound. It came from under the sink. That was for sure. This time I could tell what the sound was. It wasn't like the first sound. This time it was a sneeze. "Aaah-choo!" Just like that.

I opened the door of the cabinet under the kitchen sink. There was a little human being—sort of. He was about two feet tall, with gray hair and a dirty-looking beard, and he had a black patch over one eye. He was dressed a little like the pirates I had seen in picture books.

"Hey! Shut that door, you big baboon!" the little sort-of human shouted. "Where were you brought up, in a paper bag?"

I closed the cabinet door.

Then I stood there for a while.

Then I put water in my glass with the ice cubes in it, sat on one of the kitchen chairs, and sipped. I thought things over.

Then I went over to the kitchen sink, and knocked softly—three times—on the cabinet door.

"What is it?" said a voice from inside.

"May I come in, please?" I asked

"If you must," said the voice.

2.
When Is a Sink Not a Sink?

I opened the cabinet door. There was the little sort-of humanlike person.

"Hey! Is that ice water?" he asked.

"Yes, it is," I said.

"Give me!" He grabbed the glass, drank the water, and swallowed all the ice cubes. "More!" he said.

I fixed him another glass of ice water, and he drank that and swallowed the ice cubes too.

"Ah! That was good!" he said. "I haven't had ice water in about thirty years. Well, don't just stand there. If you're coming in, come in."

I crawled under the sink. It was a tight fit. "Do you mind if I leave the door open?" I asked the little sort-of humanlike person.

"Is there anybody else around?" he asked me.

"Not at the moment," I said.

"Well, leave it a little bit open," he said.

"Just to let some light in," I said.

"That's right," the sort-of person said. "Now what are you doing aboard my spacecraft?"

"Spacecraft? This is our kitchen sink!" I said.

"Ha! You don't know much, do you? You can't tell a space-

craft from a kitchen sink? I'll bet your grades in school aren't very good."

"They're okay," I said. "And this *is* our kitchen sink."

"It *looks* like your kitchen sink—but it is really a spacecraft. What is your name, anyway?"

"Ned."

"I am Captain Lumpy Lugo. I come from the planet Jivebone in the galaxy known as Foon-ping-baba."

"Foon-ping-baba?"

"Let me guess: You never heard of it. What do they teach you kids in school these days? Anyway, this is my spacecraft, and it looks just like your kitchen sink because I can make it look like anything I want."

"It changes its shape?"

"Yes."

"Why a kitchen sink?"

"Why not? It's a good disguise. I had to stop to fix a few things, and this is where I stopped."

"What did you do with our real kitchen sink?"

"Nothing. Your real kitchen sink is just where it always was."

I was getting confused. "But if this is not really our kitchen sink but your spacecraft—and it is where our real kitchen sink usually is—then how can our real kitchen sink be where it always was, which is the same place?"

"A very good question," Captain Lumpy Lugo said.

"It is? I didn't understand it myself, and I asked it."

"Look, this is space science—very advanced. But you can understand it. My spacecraft, which I have changed to look just like your kitchen sink, *and* your real kitchen sink, are both in the same space. Like a box inside a box, only both boxes are the same size. Understand?"

"No."

"Well, the easiest way is to show you. Pull that door shut and hold tight."

"What are you going to do?" I asked Captain Lumpy Lugo.

"We're going to take off," he said. "Now look at this screen."

There was a screen like a TV screen. I could see the whole kitchen.

"Now watch," Captain Lumpy Lugo said. "See the kitchen sink?"

I could see the kitchen sink on the screen. We were moving away from it.

"Now where did you say we were?" he asked me.

"Under the kitchen sink," I said.

"Open the door and stick your head out," Captain Lumpy Lugo said.

I opened the door, and stuck my head out. I looked around. I could see the kitchen sink where it always was, and I could see that we were in another kitchen sink, with cabinets, just like it. The kitchen sink we were in was floating in the air, above the real one.

"We *are* in a spacecraft!" I said.

"I told you," Captain Lumpy Lugo said. "Now, let's take a little ride. Better shut the door."

"A ride around the kitchen?" I asked him.

"Look at the screen."

We were passing through the wall. We went right through it—but there was no hole in the wall! Then we were outside, going up. I could see the apartment building below us. "How did we do that?" I asked Captain Lumpy Lugo.

"Space science," he said. "Now, hold on, Ned. We're going to go pretty fast. Have you ever wanted to see what it's like in outer space?"

"Always," I said.

3.
A Pirate!

"How about this spacecraft of mine!" Captain Lumpy Lugo said. "It's running smooth as a noodle!"

I could see on the screen that we were high above the earth.

"You'll have fun," the little sort-of human said. "Ned is a good name for a pirate."

"A pirate? I'm not a pirate," I said.

"You are one now," Captain Lumpy Lugo said. "You're on a pirate spaceship, with a pirate captain—what else could you be?"

"I *thought* you looked like a pirate, Captain Lumpy Lugo," I said.

"A pirate I am, Ned—and you can stop calling me Lumpy Lugo. My real name is Captain Bugbeard, Bugbeard the Pirate. I am famous for being bad."

"How bad exactly?" I asked Bugbeard the Pirate (formerly known as Captain Lumpy Lugo).

"Extremely bad, Ned, my boy," the pirate said. "If you knew of the bad things I have done, your brains would turn to pickles, your ears would fold up like wilted lettuce, and your nose would turn into a radish."

"I don't think I want to be a pirate," I said.

"Why not? Why would you not want to be a pirate? Why would anyone not want to be a pirate?" Bugbeard asked.

"I just don't," I said. "I don't think I *can* be a pirate."

"Oh, don't say that, Ned," Bugbeard said. "You can be a pirate—really you can."

"I don't want to do bad things," I said.

"You don't? Why ever not?" Bugbeard asked.

"I don't want to hurt anybody."

"How about scaring people? Scaring people is the main part of being a pirate. You wouldn't mind scaring some people, would you?"

"I'm not sure," I said.

"Well, let's do just a little bit of piracy," Bugbeard said, "just scare some people, and maybe make them give us treasure—shoe polish, or soap flakes, or whatever they have."

"Shoe polish? Soap flakes? That's treasure?" I asked.

"What would you suggest?" Bugbeard the Pirate asked.

"Gold, maybe?"

"What's gold?" Bugbeard asked. "Look, if you don't like being a pirate, I'll take you home. Would that be fair?"

"I guess that would be all right," I said.

"Good boy, Ned," Captain Bugbeard said. "Now pull that lever."

I pulled the lever. "What does this do?" I asked.

"It raises our pirate flag," Bugbeard said. "The Jolly Roger, the Skull and Bones! Every pirate flies the pirate flag—only mine says 'HAVE A NICE DAY!' and has one of those yellow smiley faces. It was the only flag I could find. I mean to get a real pirate flag someday."

4.
In Space

Well, outer space was nothing like TV! I could see a lot of stars—I expected that. What I had not expected was all the junk! There were old broken-down satellites floating around. There were hunks of metal that must have come off rockets and spaceships. There was a lot of plain old regular garbage—food wrappers, empty ice-cream containers, newspapers, and even one basketball shoe!

"Where does all this stuff come from?" I asked Bugbeard the Pirate.

"It just floats around," Bugbeard said. "This is a messy part of space."

"What are those white things?" I asked.

"Space chickens," Bugbeard said.

"There are chickens in space?" I was surprised.

"They are not the same as Earth chickens," Bugbeard said. "When we get closer, you will notice that they are about twenty feet long, and probably weigh a ton."

He was right. When we got closer, I could see that each chicken was bigger than our kitchen-sink spacecraft.

"Are these chickens dangerous?" I asked.

"What a funny question!" Bugbeard said. "Are chickens dangerous? Hee hee hee!"

CCCP

"Well, are they?" I asked.

"I don't know," Bugbeard the Pirate said. "Maybe we should get away from here. Just push that big yellow button."

"What does it do?" I asked, pushing the button.

"It makes us go *'whoosh!'*" Bugbeard said.

"Whoosh!" went the kitchen-sink spacecraft. The screen was a blur. I could feel that we were going very fast—much faster than we had gone before.

"This will take us far away from those scary chickens," Bugbeard said.

"Do you think we will be in a space battle?" I asked Bugbeard.

"Oh, I hope so!" Bugbeard the Pirate said. "I hope we get into a really big battle! There will be spaceships with big blasters, and horrible fireballs, and things blowing up, and those green beams of light that can fry you, and big, mean, nasty men with swords and iron hooks and clubs with rusty nails in them bashing us on the head."

I thought Bugbeard was looking a little green.

"And then they will chase us, and catch us, and throw us into a dark room with water dripping down the walls, and big rats, and they won't give us anything to eat, and no one will know where we are, and no one will care."

Bugbeard was looking sick now. He reached into his pocket and took out two big, white pills. They looked like the ones my father takes when he eats too much spaghetti. Bugbeard chewed the pills.

"And years will pass," Bugbeard said, "and we will still be

in that dark room with the water and the rats. And every so often, they will take us out of the room and bash us on the head with big sticks."

"Are you all right, Captain Bugbeard?" I asked.

"I think I will lie down for a while," Bugbeard said. "Watch the screen, and call me if anything unusual happens."

Bugbeard the Pirate crawled over to a little bed in a corner and lay down, muttering to himself about being chased by horrible fireballs and being bashed on the head with big sticks. I watched the screen, and wondered if Bugbeard was such a brave pirate after all. "I think his imagination is too good," I thought.

5.
We Land on a Planet

"Captain Bugbeard!" I shouted. "I think I see a planet!"

Bugbeard the Pirate had been sleeping on his little bed. He was holding a teddy bear, which did not seem very piratelike to me. When I called him he jumped up and looked at the screen.

"Good boy, Ned! It's a planet for sure," he said. "We'll land and look around. If anyone is there, we will scare the pants off them."

Bugbeard took the controls. I felt the kitchen-sink spacecraft slowing down. Soon we were on the surface of the planet.

"A perfect landing!" Bugbeard said. "Now we'll get out and have a look around."

"Is there air on this planet?" I asked. "Will we be able to breathe?"

"That is the first thing we will have to find out," Bugbeard said.

"Do you have special space-science instruments to tell whether there is air?" I asked him.

"I have one special instrument," Bugbeard said, pointing to his nose. "It is this—my educated sniffer." Bugbeard opened the door a tiny bit, and stuck his nose out. "Aah! The atmosphere is fine," he said. "Let's go!"

"Maybe we should take weapons, just in case," I said.

"We don't have any weapons," Bugbeard said.

"No weapons? No space weapons? No blasters or death rays? Not even swords?" I asked.

"I mean to get some really good pirate weapons," Bugbeard said. "I will get blasters, and those things that go '*fweet*' and make things disappear, and some really sharp swords—but I just haven't had a chance."

"What will we do if there is danger?" I asked.

"We will run back to the spacecraft," Bugbeard said. "You're a good runner, aren't you, Ned?"

"I suppose so," I said.

"On a planet this small, there won't be much gravity," Bugbeard said. "You will find that you can run as fast as a grape."

"Are grapes fast?"

"There's nothing faster."

6.
Captured by Chickens

We were walking around on the planet. It felt strange to be on another planet. All my life up to then I had lived on Earth. I can't say it was a very interesting planet. There was nothing there but a lot of big rocks.

"It's mostly rocks," I said to Bugbeard the Pirate.

"Just keep a sharp lookout," Bugbeard said. "Planets can be very surprising. And remember, any shoe polish or soap flakes we may find belong to me."

"Why are you so interested in shoe polish and soap flakes?" I asked.

"Also furniture wax and candles, and crayons," Bugbeard said. "On the planet Jivebone in the galaxy of Foon-ping-baba, these are great treasures."

"They are? What do you do with them?" I asked.

"Do? We eat them! Yum!" the pirate said. "I wish I had some soap flakes right now, and a couple of crayons—blue and green taste the best." Bugbeard the Pirate licked his lips.

"Is that why you were living under our kitchen sink at home?" I asked him.

"Of course," Bugbeard said. "Every so often, a female—I suppose it was your mother—would open the door under the sink (never dreaming that it was also the door of my spacecraft) and put in a brand-new box of soap flakes. I had to be careful not to eat too much, or she might have suspected. But it has been a long time since I had some nice shoe polish."

I found the eating habits of the people of the planet Jivebone in the Foon-ping-baba Galaxy very interesting. You learn new things all the time when you travel in space.

We wandered around on the planet, picking up small rocks and looking at big rocks. If we were not in outer

space, on a planet far away from Earth, it would have been sort of boring.

Then, Bugbeard the Pirate screamed: *"Eeeeyagh!"* Then he screamed again, *"Eeeeyagh!"*

"What is it? Why did you scream?" I asked.

"It's the space chickens!" Bugbeard said, pointing. "And they've seen us! Run! Run for your life, Ned!"

Just beyond a very big rock there *was* a flock of those giant chickens. Bugbeard the Pirate and I ran toward the kitchen-sink spacecraft as fast as we could.

Running in the weak gravity of the little planet was very different from running on Earth. I found that I could almost float. Every step took me about ten feet. It didn't take long to reach the spacecraft and get inside.

"Emergency takeoff! Hold on tight!" Bugbeard shouted. He worked the controls. Nothing happened.

"Oh, no!" Bugbeard said. "We're trapped. The chickens are smarter than I thought. They have trapped our spacecraft with some kind of chicken space-science. And they are getting closer!"

He was right. I could see them on the screen, very close, casting their chicken shadows over us.

"Are you sure we can't take off?" I asked.

"They must have some way of keeping our spacecraft from working," Bugbeard said. "See? The controls don't do anything!"

The chickens were right outside the spacecraft. All I could see on the screen was a lot of giant space-chicken legs and feet.

"What do we do now?" I asked Bugbeard.

"You have to go outside and scare the chickens," Bugbeard said.

"Me! Why me?"

"You need the experience. I have done this a thousand times," Bugbeard said.

"How can I scare them? They're five times bigger than me. What do I do, threaten them?"

"Yes! That's a good idea! Threaten them," Bugbeard said.

"Tell them if they don't let us go, we'll do some bad things to them."

"But there's nothing we can do," I said.

"The chickens don't know that!" Bugbeard said. "Go out there and outsmart them."

"I think maybe you should do it," I said. "I'll go out and threaten the next time we are captured by chickens."

"No," Bugbeard said. "It has to be you. You have to be the one to go out and deal with the chickens."

"Why?" I asked.

"Well, because I can work the spacecraft," Bugbeard said. "If the chickens get nasty, I can go for help."

"But the spacecraft won't work," I said.

"All right," Bugbeard the Pirate said. "Here's another reason. I am too scared to go out there."

7.
I Face the Chickens

"I'm going out there," I said. "But you had better be very nice to me after this."

"I will be *so* nice to you," Bugbeard said. "I will be nicer than a raisin."

"And you'd better be ready to open the door in case I have to come back inside in a hurry."

"I'll open the door faster than a—"

"—than a grape," I said.

"That's right," Bugbeard said.

"All right," I said. "I'm going. I don't know why I'm doing this."

"Because I won't," Bugbeard said.

I slipped out of the spacecraft, making no noise. The chickens were so close to me, I could feel the heat of their bodies. I could hear them breathing. They had not seen me. They were busy scratching and pecking at stuff on the ground. They did not seem dangerous. They were big, but they were chickens.

I tried talking to them. "Chickens, let us go and we will not harm you."

The chickens seemed not to pay any attention.

Then I got tough. "Chickens, I will give you one minute to

give up. After that you get the fireballs and the death blaster."

The chickens looked a little nervous, but I didn't think they understood me. I walked up to a chicken and gave it a shove. It moved out of my way. These chickens were tame.

I went back to the spacecraft. "Hey, Bugbeard!" I shouted. "You can come out. These chickens are not dangerous."

"No!" Bugbeard said from inside the spacecraft. "I won't come out. It's a trick. It's me the chickens want, not you."

"They're just regular chickens, only huge," I said. "You can come out, I promise."

"Not me," Bugbeard said. "They appear to like you—but that is no reason to think they will not jump on me as soon as I come out."

I had an idea. "Do you have any kind of rope in there?" I asked Bugbeard.

"I have some clothesline," Bugbeard said.

"Hand it out here," I said.

Bugbeard tossed the clothesline out and shut the door quickly.

I made a loop in one end of the clothesline, and swung it around my head, like a cowboy. I tossed the loop over the head of a big chicken. It squawked and struggled, but I held tight to my end of the clothesline. Soon the chicken was quiet, and would follow me wherever I led it.

I led the chicken up and down in front of the spacecraft. I knew Bugbeard would be watching on the screen.

"Hey, Bugbeard!" I shouted. "Come out here and see how tame this chicken is!"

"It's a trick," I could hear Bugbeard say inside the spacecraft. "He's waiting for me to come out so he can eat me alive."

"Watch this!" I shouted. I grabbed some feathers and climbed up onto the chicken's back. I *was* riding it like a horse. I could steer the chicken by tugging the clothesline. "Yippee! Look at me!" I shouted.

I was able to get the chicken to trot up and down, and even to fly a little.

"See? I told you there was nothing to worry about," I heard a voice say.

It was Bugbeard. He was mounted on another chicken, riding beside me. He had come out of the spacecraft when I wasn't looking.

"What?" I shouted. "You were scared to death!"

"Scared? Of these tame chickens?" Bugbeard said. "Never! Come on! Let's get them to fly higher!"

It was fun riding the flying space chickens. We flew high over the little planet. We did loops and spins and dives.

"Whoopee!" Bugbeard shouted. "This is more fun than two bananas and a peach!"

8.
Planet Explorers

"My chicken's name is Buck," Bugbeard said. "What's your chicken's name?"

"My chicken's name is ... chicken," I said.

"No! I changed my mind. I'm going to name my chicken Dobbin," Bugbeard said. "How do you like that name, Dobbin, old chicken?" He patted his chicken.

"So how did the space chickens fix the spacecraft so it wouldn't work?" I asked.

"It wasn't the chickens at all!" Bugbeard said. "I had forgotten to turn on the key. You see, there's this little key—and if you forget to turn it, nothing works."

"I was worried," I said. "I was afraid we might be stuck on this planet forever."

"The spacecraft is fine," Bugbeard said. "Oh look! Look at the blue lake! Let's fly down and explore it."

Below us there was a lake. It was very blue. And there were white hills all around it.

We guided our chickens down. Bugbeard was talking to his chicken. He had renamed it again. "Whoa, Thunder!" he said. "That's a good chicken, Thunder!"

The hills around the lake were covered with snow. It was really nice snow—just like snow on Earth, except it wasn't

cold. It was warm! It was just like snow in every other way. It was white, it was powdery, and it was slippery. But when you touched it, it was as warm as grass on a summer's day.

We tied our chickens to a rock. "Stay here, like a good chicken, Old Whitey," Bugbeard said. He had renamed his chicken again. "This is good snow," he said. "Let's slide!"

It was good snow. We slid all the way down to the edge of the lake. Sliding on warm snow, once I got used to it, was even better than sliding on cold snow.

The lake was frozen solid! When I touched it, the ice felt almost as warm as the snow. "Why is the snow warm, and the ice nearly as warm?" I asked Bugbeard.

"I'd say that water freezes at a much higher temperature on this planet," Bugbeard said. "This ice looks pretty thick. I think it's safe to go sliding on the lake. But first, we have to name the lake."

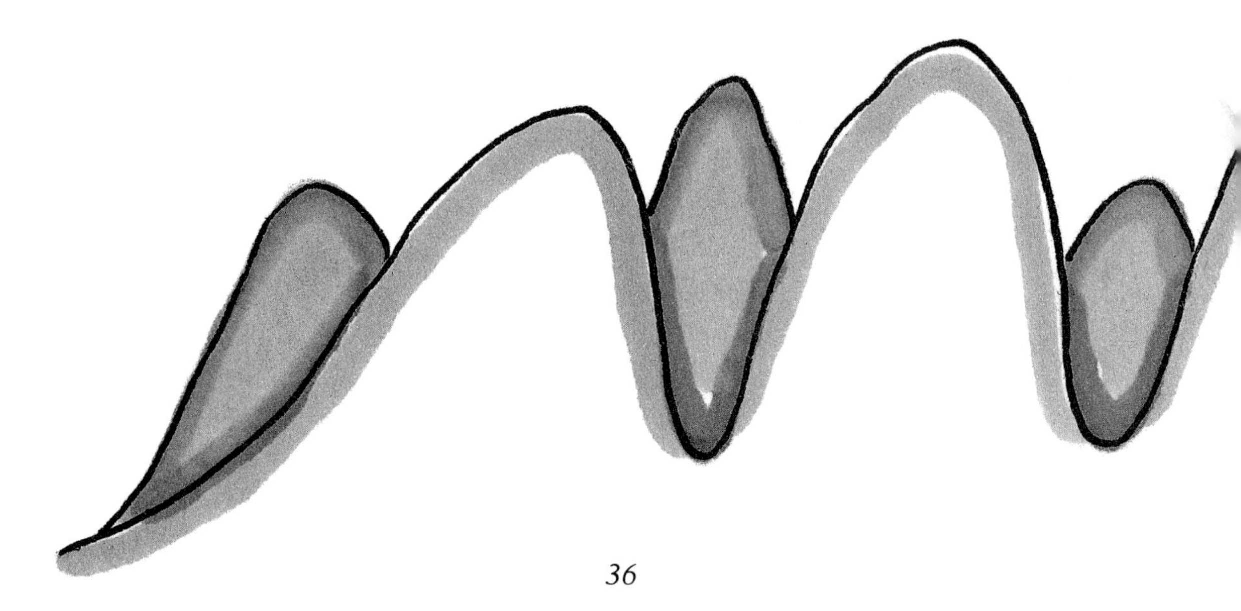

"We do?" I asked.

"Of course," Bugbeard said. "We are explorers. Except for chickens, nobody has ever been here before. We get to name everything. Now stand up straight, and salute."

Bugbeard made me stand up straight with one hand on top of my head and a finger in one ear. That is the Foon-ping-baba salute.

"I name this lake 'Lake Bugbeard,'" Bugbeard said. "I name these hills 'the Bugbeard Hills.' And I name this planet 'Bugbeard.'"

"You're naming everything after yourself!" I said.

"All right, all right," Bugbeard said. "I name that hill over there 'Ned Feldman's Hill.' Are you satisfied?"

"Show me the hill that's named after me, again," I said.

"That one there," Bugbeard said. "See, the little one?"

"Yes."

"Good. Now let's slide on the lake."

9.
In Trouble

"You do know how to slide on a lake, don't you, Ned?" Bugbeard asked me.

"Um ... no," I said.

"When sliding down a hill, you sit down or lie down. When sliding on a lake, you stand up. You slide on your feet. It's skating without skates. Understand?"

"Sure," I said.

"Of course you do. It's as easy as a grapefruit," Bugbeard said.

It *was* as easy as a grapefruit. We had fun sliding on the solid surface of Lake Bugbeard, and got almost all the way across when Bugbeard shouted, "Oh no!"

"What now?"

"Oh, my fingers, ears, and nose! Slide, Ned, slide as fast as you can! We have to get back to the chickens, and get away from here."

"Why? What did you see this time?" I asked.

"Yeti! There's a yeti here! Don't waste time talking! Slide!"

We were sliding across the lake as fast as we could. Bugbeard looked really scared.

"What is a yeti?" I asked.

"Oh, no! It's following us!" Bugbeard moaned.

I looked behind us. Sure enough something was after us.
"That's a yeti?" I asked.
"That's a yeti."
"It sure is horrible."
"Yes, it is."
"What will it do if it catches us?"
"I'm not going to stay and find out."
The yeti was the scariest thing I had ever seen. Not only was it the scariest thing I had ever seen in real life, it was also the scariest thing I had ever seen on TV or in a movie, or in an ad for a movie I was not allowed to see because it was too scary. It was also the scariest thing I had ever heard of or imagined.
I am not going to tell what the yeti looked like. It was too scary.
We reached the shore of the lake. The yeti was pretty far behind us. We could slide on ice better than it could. But the yeti was faster at climbing up the snow-covered hill than we were. Our head start got smaller and smaller. By the time we reached the chickens and hopped on their backs, the yeti was just behind us.
"Fly, chickens, fly!" Bugbeard shouted. As the chickens took to the air, the yeti was snatching at their feet. He just missed grabbing my chicken's foot.
We went higher and higher. I could see the yeti below us. It was running fast. It was following us!
"The yeti will get tired, won't it?" I called to Bugbeard.
"A yeti never gets tired," Bugbeard shouted from his chicken. "Our only hope is to reach the spacecraft and take off before he gets there."

10.
Out of Trouble

We made it to the spacecraft with the yeti close behind. We turned our chickens loose and got inside as fast as we could.

"Quick! Take off!" I shouted.

"Oh, my whiskers, teeth, and toes!" Bugbeard cried. "The spacecraft isn't working."

The yeti had almost reached us. "Turn the key! Turn the key!" I shouted.

"Of course!" Bugbeard said. "The key! Silly me!"

When Bugbeard got the spacecraft started, the yeti was already pounding on the outside. When I looked at the screen, it was filled with the yeti's scary face.

"Take off! Take off!" I shouted.

"We are lifting off now," Bugbeard said. "Look at that yeti. He certainly looks angry. On the other hand, he might just want to be friends. Still, I think the safe thing to do is to get out of here as fast as we can."

"I agree," I said.

Soon we were cruising in outer space. "Well," Bugbeard said, "I am quite hungry after all that sliding and running from the yeti. It is time to break out the emergency snacks." Bugbeard opened a little box that was taped to the wall. "I

have two crayons—one blue and one green. Which flavor would you like?"

"Is that all you've got, crayons?" I asked.

"They're still fairly fresh," Bugbeard said.

"I'll take blue," I said.

"Good," Bugbeard said. "Green is my favorite."

"Next time we go into space, I'm going to bring some crackers and cheese or something," I said.

"Suit yourself," Bugbeard said, munching his green crayon. "Where shall we go now?"

"I think you'd better take me home," I said. "My mother and father will be wondering where I am."

"All right! Homeward bound!" Bugbeard said.

11.
Home Again

Once again the kitchen-sink spacecraft passed through the wall and into the kitchen, like a ghost in a movie. Then Bugbeard made it hover above the real kitchen sink, and then we sort of melted into it until there was only one kitchen sink.

"Tell me again how we do that?" I asked Bugbeard.

"As I said, it's space science," Bugbeard said. "The spacecraft is exactly the same size and shape as the kitchen sink, and when we fit it into exactly the same space, there appears to be only one thing."

"But how can two things exist in the same space?" I asked.

"That's the scientific part," Bugbeard said.

"It sounds more like magic," I said.

"No, this is magic," Bugbeard said. "Pick a card, any card." Bugbeard had taken a deck of cards out of his pocket.

I picked a card. It was the four of diamonds.

"Now, don't show it to me," Bugbeard said. "Put the card back in the deck."

"This is your card, right?" Bugbeard showed me the three of clubs.

"My card was the four of diamonds," I said.

"Oh," Bugbeard said.

"I'm going to go to my room for a while," I said. "I feel like drawing some pictures of yetis on the margins of my homework."

"Fine. I'll stay here," Bugbeard said.

"I'll bring you some shoe polish later," I said.

I climbed out from under the kitchen sink. There I was in my old familiar kitchen again. It felt strange to be back home after traveling in space. I didn't really know how long I had been gone. I wondered if my parents had been worried.

Then I heard the key in the lock of the front door. It was my mother and father, coming home.

"Hi, Mom and Dad!" I said. "Did you have a nice time?"

"Yes," my mother said. "When you are older you may come along when we go to see professional wrestling. We had a very good time. Did you have a nice afternoon?"

"I did," I said. "It turns out that our kitchen sink is really a spacecraft, and a space pirate lives in it. We went to outer space, and we visited a planet, and we rode giant chickens, and we slid in warm snow, and we were chased by a yeti."

My mother and father smiled at each other. "Well, Ned, it sounds as though you had an exciting time."

"I did," I said. "I had an exciting time. I hope you don't mind that I went to outer space without asking you first."

"It's perfectly all right, Ned," my father said.

"And you won't mind if I go again?"

"Of course not," my father said. "You may have adventures in space whenever you wish."

My favorite president
is Gerald Ford. He
was President after
Richard Nixon. He
was a nice man,
and he often
tripped and fell
down. When he
played golf, he
would often hit
people in the
head.